We All Go Traveling By

BUS STOP

Written by **Sheena Roberts**
Illustrated by **Siobhan Bell**
Sung by **Fred Penner**

Barefoot Books
step inside a story

I spy with my little eye,
You can hear with your little ear,

A yellow school bus goes *beep-beep-beep.*

And we all go traveling by, bye-bye,
And we all go traveling by.

**I spy with my little eye,
You can hear with your little ear,**

A bright red truck goes *rumble-rumble-rumble.*

A yellow school bus goes *beep-beep-beep.*

And we all go traveling by, bye-bye,
And we all go traveling by.

I spy with my little eye,
You can hear with your little ear,

A long blue train goes *chuff-chuff-chuff.*

A bright red truck goes *rumble-rumble-rumble.*

A yellow school bus goes *beep-beep-beep.*

And we all go traveling by, bye-bye,
And we all go traveling by.

I spy with my little eye,
You can hear with your little ear,

A shiny pink bike goes *ring-ring-ring.*

A long blue train goes *chuff-chuff-chuff.*

A bright red truck goes *rumble-rumble-rumble.*

A yellow school bus goes *beep-beep-beep.*

And we all go traveling by, bye-bye,
And we all go traveling by.

I spy with my little eye,
You can hear with your little ear,

A little green boat goes *chug-a-lug-a-lug.*

A shiny pink bike goes
ring-ring-ring.

A long blue train goes
chuff-chuff-chuff.

A bright red truck goes *rumble-rumble-rumble*.

A yellow school bus goes *beep-beep-beep*.

And we all go traveling by, bye-bye,
And we all go traveling by.

I spy with my little eye,
You can hear with your little ear,

A big white plane goes *neeeeeeee-oww.*

A little green boat goes
chug-a-lug-a-lug.

A shiny pink bike goes *ring-ring-ring*.

A long blue train goes *chuff-chuff-chuff*.

A bright red truck goes *rumble-rumble-rumble*.

A yellow school bus goes *beep-beep-beep*.

And we all go traveling by, bye-bye,
And we all go traveling by.

I spy with my little eye,
You can hear with your little ear,

A fast orange car goes
   vroom-vroom-vroom.

A big white plane goes *neeeeeeee-oww.*

A little green boat goes *chug-a-lug-a-lug.*

A shiny pink bike goes *ring-ring-ring.*

A long blue train goes *chuff-chuff-chuff*.
A bright red truck goes *rumble-rumble-rumble*.
A yellow school bus goes *beep-beep-beep*.

And we all go traveling by, **bye-bye**,
And we all go traveling by.

I spy with my little eye,
You can hear with your little ear,

Two purple shoes go *tap-tap-tap*.

A fast orange car goes *vroom-vroom-vroom*.

A big white plane goes *neeeeeeee-oww*.

A little green boat goes *chug-a-lug-a-lug.*
A shiny pink bike goes *ring-ring-ring.*
A long blue train goes *chuff-chuff-chuff.*
A bright red truck goes *rumble-rumble-rumble.*
A yellow school bus goes *beep-beep-beep.*

And we all go traveling by, bye-bye,
And we all go traveling by.

I spy with my little eye,
You can hear with your little ear,

A loud silver bell goes *ding-a-ling-a-ling.*

And we all start another school day, **hooray!**

And we all start another school day!

Traveling By!

A bright red truck

A yellow school bus

A long blue train

A big white plane

A shiny pink bike

A fast orange car

A little green boat

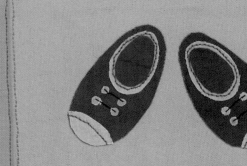

Two purple shoes

For Charlie and Jake — S. R.

For Vini — S. B.

Barefoot Books
2067 Massachusetts Ave
Cambridge, MA 02140

First published in the United States of America by Barefoot Books, Inc in 2003
This paperback edition first published in 2019. All rights reserved

Graphic design by Barefoot Books, UK and Mayfly Design, Minneapolis
Color separation by B & P International, Hong Kong
Printed in China on 100% acid-free paper by Printplus, Ltd
This book was typeset in GrilledCheese and Billy
The illustrations were prepared using hand-dyed cotton sheets

ISBN 978-1-78285-988-8

Library of Congress Cataloging-in-Publication Data is available under LCCN 2004017943

5 7 9 8 6 4

Go to *www.barefootbooks.com/travelingby* to access
your audio singalong and video animation online.